Only When There is a Y in the Day

1st Edition

A long short story by

Antonia Cordobes

Tony Wil

Only When There is a Y in the Day

Edited by Debz Hobbs-Wyatt
Formatting by Polgarus Studio

Acknowledgements

Thanks to the NHS, care workers and all frontline staff in these unprecedented times.

Thanks to the scientists for the vaccine.

To Hickleton golf club for allowing us locals to walk the course and discover the peaceful beauty we had not seen.

To all those in entertainment for which this book originally started as a play. Requires just 6 of you to conform with the original guidelines.

To Debz for guiding me.

To my friend Locky who said he had to read it twice it was so good. I think he wants a pint when the pubs reopen!

To all my other friends who read it and were surprisingly complementary.

To Cathy who puts up with me and agrees with all the above.

To Captain Sir Tom Moore who told an interviewer "Even at a 100 no one can stop us dreaming". RIP 02/02/2021. A legend.

Friday, March 20th, 2020

I could never have imagined what a roller coaster ride my life would take between now and January 1st, 2021. Lockdown, hoedown, or just plain down, somehow, we try to survive.

I, Mary Claire Cavendish, faithful and loving wife to John for twenty-seven years, was invited by him to go to a solicitor's meeting at 2pm.

We owned two nursing homes and I worked part time to get my tax-free allowance. It was worth it as I gave good advice and did check the bank statements. I qualified as a nurse which was useful in the early days of the business.

He was upset to miss his afternoon golf. I helped at the club sometimes for meals. The cricket club recommended me as I was the quintessential queen of cricket teas. I soon got the nickname of MCC – my initials. They reckoned I increased the crowd when they saw I was down for teas in the local mag. I did have other attributes and the warm weather was an excuse to show off. Well men have bats/clubs and balls and we women – *we have charisma.*

The cricket season was only a month away and friendly

games were already plotted, usually near a good pub. Are not all of them?

We drove to the solicitor's office. Arriving early, we were greeted by Rebecca, the wife of Percy Dickinson whose practice it was – a one-man band who had fallen out with his previous partners and never looked back. Rebecca only worked on a Friday for the same reasons I was employed. Every Friday as part of her work she had her nails and toes professionally painted. This time they were in the colours of a horse she had backed at Cheltenham. Yes – some women do gamble.

She greeted us both warmly; after all we did pay the bills. I reminded her about our monthly dinner party the following day. Percy's premises were three rooms in a block for commercial use on an industrial estate. Adequate and not too expensive. His full-time secretary had every Friday afternoon off. His assistant in all legal matters was simply employed but would move on once there was no hope of becoming a partner. Another would replace him fresh from university no doubt.

We were ushered into his room and he sat behind his desk, more like a judge than a solicitor. Suit and tie and a several piles of files that hid his larger-than-average gut. We declined a drink as we had just had lunch at the golf club. Percy was a regular golfer as was my John, but Rebecca and I were just social members, ideal for the nineteenth hole. He got straight to the point. It was one of his infuriating habits and I doubted if Rebecca enjoyed much foreplay that us girls simply adore. Then we can say no if we like.

Percy announced the injunction against the manageress at Starling Nursing Home was now a no go. John was furious but understood. Mrs Daylark, nicknamed Mrs Nightingale by all her staff, had ruthlessly declared her nursing home a fortress in early March. Gates padlocked after two caravans were placed on the lawn. No staff allowed out. No visitors. Food and drugs dropped off at the gates. Doctors only allowed in. John was refused entry. Family, husbands and wives of staff all issuing court orders to see them. She had found some old PPE equipment in the cellar. Not suitable but better than nothing. She claimed her great- great grandmother had books on how to defeat a pandemic and was sticking to it.

Percy explained to us that the pandemic was spreading faster than anyone imagined. A lockdown from the 23rd – like many other countries in Europe – has been announced for the UK. Percy rambled on about how his work was mounting up and would have to work here all weekend but would not miss the dinner party. Finally, he gave his advice via some observations.

"You ought to be grateful for her actions, laundry done in-house, good allotments to use," John muttered, "two have died of natural causes and she will not let anyone else in."

I knew he was thinking about the lost income, so I reminded him the other one was full. That was cheaper for the residents to afford, many part-time staff, some from abroad. The food was cheaper to buy and John had access as did family and friends. It was run like a holiday camp with standards much lower than Starling but gave us a very healthy income. More of a care home than Starling that had more qualified nursing staff. He gave us his bill as he politely pointed out he would be working from home from the 23rd. I decided to pay the large amount as he would be at my dinner party the next evening. He advised us to take no further action or wasted letters as some had already rung up to cancel their actions against Starling Nursing Home.

As we left, it was a coincidence that the other two on my guest list were in the waiting room. David Jones was a likeable rogue who had done time for swindling many people. He served time but had made millions. He was sat opposite Pamela Patricia Elijah: a Windrush baby who everyone called Pretty. As a youngster her beauty was reflected in her nickname, but age was catching up with her. They both lived next to each other in a nearby cul de sac. Immaculately presented, with the best hairdo of us all. A warm and lovely spiritual lady, if only David thought the same. She also had a wicked sense of humour which enhanced the dinner parties, especially sitting next to David. I noticed she had two files on her lap. Our eyes met. I reminded her about the dinner party. Pretty responded by pointing at her files and simply saying "House completion." It was more a statement of fact. She worked for a local estate agency. I guessed she also had a file for Percy for her elderly parents hoping for compensation. The Windrush scandal was common knowledge. I turned my attention to David.

"And what exactly is a rascal like you doing here?"

David Jones was a con man extraordinaire, unbelievably wealthy yet a bit of a recluse. An old-fashioned Dandy of a man with a twinkle in his eye. Pretty fancied him, but David only had his eyes on me. Of course, I flirted a little, but he had no chance. He was interesting company and John and Percy seemed to respect the scoundrel. Rebecca despised him. David eventually smiled almost luringly at me regardless of John being so close.

"I have come to pay my bill, as a few weeks ago Percy told me I could now start a business." He smiled triumphantly as though he had broken my guard for him. I would save my comments for the dinner party.

We lived in the north of England near Doncaster. I was a Yorkshire girl, but my husband came from Ware on the A10 north of London which always brought a chorus of "Where?" I love cooking and dinner parties. I love my husband, my garden, my house. I plan holidays and had two lined up soon. John was happy if there was a golf course close by. I love shopping and the internet is an alcoholic mirage for "checkout here". It is a good thing we can spend as we like. My two children, Elizabeth and Mathew, live with their respective husband and wife in Basingstoke and Wimbledon. They each have one child, Stephanie and Roger. Elizabeth's husband is Charlie and Mathew's wife is Charlotte, easier for young-looking grandma to remember. They all have jobs and life seems good down south. In fact, life is good up north.

Saturday, March 21st

Saturday March 21st will be remembered for the uncertainty we all felt.

The atmosphere was quieter than usual. We looked at each other as though on death row but somehow thinking we would all be okay. It was surreal and I now knew what people must have thought in September, 1939. This time the enemy was invisible. We had no idea that at Oxford they had already been working on a vaccine for over two months. *Oh, why are we so wise after the event?* The six of us are sat at our usual seats. No social distancing yet.

John was quiet compared to the raucous behaviour of David. John is ten years older than me but thinks he looks younger. He is in charge of the table, and keeps the drinks flowing. Rebecca is an absolute angel, except when talking to David. She helps in the kitchen and always flashes her nails and later toenails. She's forever looking at them, and hardly ever pays attention to the topic of conversation. This makes her so entertaining without her realizing why. We three girls always commend each one's attire, although the men think differently, we do not care. We often look at fashion books while the men talk. Rebecca always makes an entrance, dresses as she likes, which invites comments. After a few glasses of champagne, or prosecco these days, wow does she change. That is when the night gets interesting, but Percy spoils the fun by taking her home. Nothing better than watching others get inebriated.

As for me I am the *hostess with the mostest.* I keep the party going and love the extra glass of wine. The conversation is often erratic but sex, drugs, rock and roll some of the topics. It is ironic that in our group, as far as I know, no one takes drugs, alcohol seems sufficient and the rest is normal!

The evening was broken by phone calls from Elizabeth and Mathew. They wished all was well and would miss seeing each other. Finished with love you, after John had a brief word. I managed not to cry as the thought of this lockdown was dawning on us all.

One of my qualities is to remember conversations. The evening went something like this.

John started by stating, “You had a busy Friday, Percy?”

David was quick to add, “Yes, I served my sentence for fraud and have had seven years without being a company director.”

Rebecca joined in with hate in her voice. “Oh, bet you have thought of making money out of this pandemic.”

Pretty looked longingly at David as he simply smiled and retorted, “Wait and see.”

“Have you got supplies of PPE coming?” Percy enquired of us.

John responded, "Absolute chaos, we are on the case, I think the local sewing group are on with the job. We need masks, gowns, face shields, hand sanitiser. Only a few supplies currently available."

I produced snacks before dinner started. I thought David might be useful.

"Can you get us, PPE, David? After all, you are renowned for your contacts home and abroad."

I asked the simple question as his furtive eyes and uneasiness in his chair suggested he was up to his old tricks. He responded by denying any contacts but closed in on Pretty. "I am sure you can make some with your skills."

I was taken aback then as Pretty demanded the detailed requirements of PPE. I had no idea but pretended I did. John did help me out, but he, too, simply said he would get his secretary to email Pretty with PPE specifications.

Pretty amusingly said, "PPE stands for me Pamela Patricia Elijah" as Rebecca wandered off David gave his version of PPE "Part Paid Endowment".

I looked at John and Percy to see who would be next as I was still thinking.

John gave me his cue "Putting Practise Extended" to which I instantly joined in with "Pretty Poor Excuse".

Percy was smiling but added "Painful Party Entertainment" as Rebecca returned not knowing the flow.

Rebecca stood there looking at her gorgeous nails and proclaimed to everyone "Perfectly Painted Extensions" waiting for admiration. All she got was an explosion of laughter. Drinks replenished and after a short pause the party continued.

Percy tackled John. "How is Donald doing in London?"

That's John's identical twin brother.

"Very busy with his work, I expect he is trying to source PPE as a civil servant. I will be in touch with him next week."

I remember serving the three-course meal. Drinks flowed as usual. Rebecca started on orange juice and later switched to champagne. As they always brought champagne I did not mind. But we felt obliged to open a second bottle. Pretty brought chocolates to go with the coffee or brandy at the end.

The tight sod, David, brought a half-bottle of cheap wine from the car boot, but he never drank that.

We did watch the late news. It was very bleak.

David seemed a little drunk and I was surprised when John and Percy asked him about his previous accounts in a Swiss Bank and his time in prison. I was even more surprised, after yet another large glass of red wine disappeared down David's clacker, he volunteered how the accounts were set up.

Boasting about his exploits and not caring, as it was all a thing of the past, he said. "Only two years till I get my pension!"

Rebecca swiftly said, "On top of your bloody millions, you deserve nothing."

"I served my time and I thought calling myself Mr Prewdential was a fair way of taking investments over a ten-year term. It was only when the maturity date neared, did my problems start. They did not miss £20 or £30 a month. Moved houses four times before they caught me. Did very well out of it."

Percy concluded, "You hid it in Switzerland, then Andorra and the Cayman Islands, clever lad only to hand back a small proportion."

Pretty admired him. "Is the cash still under your bed? Why not let me find out..." her flashing eyes trying to lure him. Percy joined in.

"6000 people conned over ten years x £20 minimum per month, even allowing for dropouts, cancellations that is an awful lot of money. No wonder you could afford to move and keep many millions, the courts were far too believing about where the money had gone."

David felt pleased with himself. "Paid your bills, Percy, and my expensive holidays. I was careful, mainly went for the older people. Just had to check the deaths column and intuition. I travelled a lot."

Rebecca instinctively proclaimed, "You should have gone skiing and met an avalanche."

David searched for a reply but before he could respond, Pretty put her hands on his legs. His napkin fell onto the floor. David slowly went under the table to retrieve his napkin. He was there longer than necessary. Rebecca was now showing more than she should and I decided to join in the fun. My legs are well worth looking at and I loved to flirt with David. When he resurfaced Percy announced it was time to go home.

David boldly said, "Dates of birth and house numbers then bingo legs 11, always end up with that."

Everyone ignored him not knowing what the hell he was talking about.

We had coffee and mints first, but David and John stopped on the alcohol. It felt like the last supper. There was a poor rendition of 'We'll meet again don't know when…' coats were put on, and luckily, all lived within walking distance.

David as ever, was drunk enough to offer to sleep with me as the cold air came in the house.

I told him no chance as we all had got used to his harmless comments.

"I will only sleep with you when there is a Y in the day."

David's final departing words a relief, as I could now close the door and hope he would go back for coffee with Pretty.

July

Food banks, daily records of deaths by Covid and a worsening situation abounds. Walking and finding Zoom was not an ice cream. Thursday clapping for the NHS and Carers, VE Day and Sir Captain Tom. Downing Street updates and where is Dominic Cummings? Will he stay or will he go!

So much to talk about.

The next dinner party was planned for July, 11th – a week after Super Saturday, the day football returned. It was changed to the 25th as David had to isolate after a trip to Turkey. There seemed a false sense of relief as the virus went into retreat. Summer was here, but how could we forget the glorious lockdown weather. The Starling Nursing Home had a new sealed conservatory adjoining the home. The covered window gave visitors shelter and allowed them to talk to their loved ones without contact. The cost made John wince even though it had been sponsored by families of the residents. I got some money back for our cancelled holidays. Flight refunds – we gave up on and accepted vouchers for the future. John spent more time in our garden. Grumpy with no golf for a long time the trips were replaced with garden centre visits and more walks. The garden did look resplendent. Areas that had been neglected were cleared of weeds and new bulbs or plants made colourful additions. The overhanging branches from the estate behind were trimmed that can best be described as a crew cut. More sun and better views, even the neighbours were happier. We discovered more about them as well as sharing a toast and a laugh occasionally. The local spirit seemed to flourish everywhere.

We ate outside most of April and May. I cancelled our home help and bought a new iron and ironing board. Drinking at home rather than at the club. We did jobs around the house that had needed doing for years. Kitchen cupboards and handles repaired. We spent an hour waiting at the tip several times, but it did not seem to matter. We listened to the radio more and we started big jigsaws – 1000 pieces that took a month to do. The Classic FM was particularly difficult. I did insist on one view only then I hid the picture, much harder to do. John thought doing between three and six pieces a day a good effort for him. I would do more not that it mattered. Finally, we celebrated when completed, then bought another of the world. I wondered if we were naturally masochistic, but life goes on slowly and pensively in this *unprecedented* moment in time. This new watchword on every politician's lips.

There was one particular day that will remain with me for ever. Friday, May 22nd.

We agreed to take a picnic to the golf club. We walked the course first as did a few others. I had never done this before. I learnt about Dog legs, Whiteman's stream (allegedly took fourteen shots), the valley of death and other silly names. The sun shone and the slight breeze made for a wonderful time. Eventually, we found a flat area near the infamous seventh hole. I laid out the blanket and we kicked off our sandals. It was time to relax and eat. We ate some nuts as he got the corkscrew to do the honours. The noise of the cork popping was joy to my ears. He had a cold beer from the cool bag, where the wine bottle retreated to after filling my glass. Some pâté and prawns wrapped in smoked salmon, washed down with our drinks, life felt great. John scoured the course and eventually I had to have the golf lecture. It was no surprise as rumours about this hole were disbelieved by us non-players. Here begins the lesson.

Not being a golfer, I had to endure the frailties of this hole. John gesticulated and pointed to the fifth and tenth flags, explaining to me they were the only other players who could witness where the ball had finished on this par 3 seventh hole. He opened another beer. I preferred the white wine. Of course, sometimes we get the odd spectator, John continued now immersed in his story. I was not going to stop him now but wondered what the seven-step contraption was near the driving area. Sitting up, we decided on the sandwiches, eating, and looking at the view in silent admiration. Oh, it was so hot he opened a third beer and refilled my wine glass. The cool bag was very useful, and I was beginning to feel warm and happy. A young couple walked by and we acknowledged each other. They went up the steps and came down sniggering and giving us strange looks. We sat and admired the view, the sloping land and the top of the Clubhouse in the distance.

Several dogs and owners at different points of the course. There was no timetable now, just the late afternoon sun attacking our sun cream. It was a moment in time that I wanted to stay still. I had put on a white top, far too hot for a bra. My tennis-type skirt ideal for the breeze and John's wandering eye. He was dressed in a T-shirt and shorts. Summer was early and the birds and sounds seductive to the ear. The grass not as green as normal, cows mooing in the distance, birds flying by in small numbers. Rabbits chased each other through some trees. Idyllic and no one to check how long we had been here. Exercising was allowed but time constrained. If anyone asked, we had just arrived.

I was waiting for John's move as I expertly tempted him with a kiss and my wandering hands. Much to my annoyance he preferred to explain about this wooden obelisk with seven steps. He looked around the golf course and it was very quiet now, nobody close. He continued his story from earlier, luckily, I had been listening and remembered the hole was a blind one when you teed off.

"It was Dick Dastardly that had this built so that when you play a shot your partner can watch from the top of this and see where the ball is on the green, what he did not realise that after playing your shot if you ran up quick enough you might see the ball finish, yourself!"

That was not his real name but when Dick Goodenough died, he had money left in his will to make this so the shot could be witnessed. He practised a shot and ran up to the top and pretended it had just rolled in. I remembered him looking at me triumphantly even though he had never had a hole in one.

He was looking down at me and I wondered why so many people had nicknames. I was getting bored; I simply wanted him to make love to me, right here, right now.

But he continued…

"When Dick Dastardly played his shot there were shouts of joy from one of the other greens but he was not convinced. Perhaps a bird or a hand of God, Maradona style, had somehow spirited it into the hole."

I was bemused but happy that John found it all so amusing. The wine was having its effect. The moment of truth had arrived.

"Come here!" he instructed to the bottom of the stairs. I obeyed. "When you get to the top you will see the poem he had done, just go and read."

The inscription at the bottom simply read *Staircase to Heaven* with an arrow pointing upwards. He watched me climb the seven steps and I hoped he got a good eyeful. Was a golf story more important than my desires? But duty called. At the top was a seaside-type telescope in one corner. It had out of order on it – *Repair Shop Pending*, one of my favourite programmes. I moved to the centre but where was this poem? I could now see the seventh green clearly. The view was exhilarating *after a short staircase to heaven* as the inscription said. There were avenue of fir trees and then silver birches inviting us to walk through. In the distance were Lowry-type figures and a dog. One had to bend over and grip two bike-like handlebars to read the poem sticking out in the open. The glass case protected it on wooden supports that stretched back to the obelisk. The leather saddle-like support on my waist made it comfortable. It felt like the famous sequence on the *Titanic* except in a different slightly embarrassing position.

I was bent over, the soft warm breeze travelled over my whole body. My skirt moving like butterfly wings. It was not as intense as the Marilyn Monroe moment, but I hoped John was admiring me. I started to read, the adrenalin and pleasure of the poem took me to the meaning of life.

Please take only four minutes others are waiting

Welcome dear Lady to the fairway of heaven
Hope you are ready for my club, the trusty seven
With trees to the right and a brook
Oh yes, sometimes better to hook
Sweetly I struck my teed-up ball
Wondering where this beauty might fall
It just missed the brook, a big hit for my size
Saw it bounce once, straight at the prize
We shrugged our shoulders and prayed to be near
Gleeful shouts from out of view, we did hear
Who shot that? was the noise loud and clear
The cry came out, get 'em in, we want beer
Fair maiden you are now in for a surprise
For stay still, close your eyes, I will summarise
Hope it is your partner who will take you from behind
Or was it the guest member you had on your mind.

By the time I had finished the poem, the steps behind could only be John. I hung on to the handles as he gently moved his hands up my skirt and swiftly pulled my pants down. I surrendered willingly, gazing at the landscape. I had to take a tighter grip as fingering was followed by his mighty club. My breasts he opened to the world, but I did not care. Caressing my nipples as he pounded me into submission. We grunted and groaned but four minutes was enough. The glow I felt could not be explained. The dog-leg climax, I think I could get into golf, was so worth the wait. I wondered what sort of man Dick was, a dreamer no doubt.

"So few get a hole in one like that," I smiled at his Cheshire grin as I teased him. He only had to look at me to see the happiness and smirk on my face. I did not care if anyone else had been watching. We lay down and finished the bottle of wine while he had the last beer. It was Chardonnay, I renamed it Shagaday. We were both so happy and full of life, *oh for more lockdowns.* I asked him what happened when two couples played the same hole?

"We allow eight minutes." I could not stop laughing and we rolled together off the blanket.

The evening sun was low by the time we got home. Our hands tightly knit, we had to walk past the road called Lady Mary View. John remarked he had already had that view and I gave an embarrassing smile. I gave him my rendition of two verses Dick Dastardly had missed off. I now appreciated his nickname. May the force be with me, I was on another planet.

For those that titter and complain about such a crazy sexy plot
Remember, we are only alive because of someone else's playful shot.

John laughed very loud. Brilliant, I will ask the committee to have it added. I begged him not to say it was my idea. We had a night cap on the patio. We played some songs on our old vinyl player, taking it in turns to choose, even the neighbours asked us to turn it up. He played Whitney Houston 'I Wanna Dance with Somebody'... "I wanna to feel the heat with somebody, yeh dance with somebody like you, with somebody who loves me..." Our eyes met as we danced, our hands were tight together and I knew he still loved me. We played several more and finished yet another bottle between us. I thought of the song and began to sing gently 'Days I remember all my life'. I insisted it had to be played. We danced again the last of the night, he looked into my beautiful eyes.

The candle was at the end it flickered defiantly but I blew it out. Bedtime beckoned and we slept the sleep of contentment as if Covid was no longer.

Saturday, July 25th

It had been a long time since the six of us met together. Summer had arrived but the spring had been simply sensational. Percy and Rebecca always arrived first. This time he brought an expensive Moet & Chandon champagne. Times were hard for us and I had a cheap prosecco from Asda in the fridge. Pretty presented herself in a beautiful Barbadian summery outfit. I felt aggrieved I could not now afford a steel band. The chocolates were exquisitely made by her. I had to have an early one with my gin and tonic. David was not far behind her with his usual cheap half-bottle that was only suitable for cooking. I poured it straight into the fruit cocktail as I had waited for it deliberately. We were all sat outside and a reasonable distance apart. We were essentially three bubbles anyway. They had all brought their own plates, cutlery and glasses for drinks. I had sanitiser on a stand that everyone used. John was busy serving drinks as Pretty and David sat close together. John and I had our chairs well away from the four of them. Rebecca started on an orange juice but swiftly had a fruit cocktail by its side. The boys all had beers. Pretty had a cocktail as did I after my gin and tonic. Rebecca joined me in the kitchen to help with some snacks first and put the champagne in the fridge for later. When she returned and we three girls had done the usual "how beautiful we all looked", David got the party off to a sticky start. Rebecca did ask for it though. Her nails and toenails in the NHS colours and the only one wearing a mask to begin with also in NHS colours. Her brightly coloured outfit was worthy of comment.

"Rebecca, darling, you look like a strutting peacock."

"A beautiful peacock at that," Pretty was quick to point out. "And I made the mask," she proudly announced.

Rebecca was clearly itching to have a go at David, and she did not disappoint... "As for you, David, you need a mask to hide you from society."

At this point I tried to calm things down and asked David where he had been all these months. We'd hardly seen him.

"Went to Turkey just before the first lockdown and stayed two weeks. Easier than I thought to get back, no one at airports and plenty of room on the plane."

He did not seem to want to say more but Percy and John had other ideas.

"Oh yes, David, I have got the company details for you and Pretty is your secretary, Yes, you do need two to form a company you know." Percy was in his solicitor mode. Why do people always talk business at parties? Even John asked if he had any contacts for PPE to which David smiled and ended the conversation by saying he was working on it. Pretty still looked at David with her legs and bosom on display in such a seductive manner. I felt sorry for her as he blatantly ignored her to a degree and eyeballed me. At this point I announced that the royal 'We' were raising money for the local food banks. It was all my doing. I hope you all have money on you, no cheques from David and he knew I meant it. Now then any Member of Parliament, Trump, the word Covid and any swear words £1 into the kitty. I gave Pretty a book and pen to write down any miscreants.

"Going to be a bloody quiet evening," John was quick to point out.

"Is bloody a swear word?" Pretty asked, pen at the ready.

"I think, if so Pretty will need a second pen," Percy added.

John was more intent on Percy now. "Your bloody pen knows how to make pretty big bills, as well as Covid crippling me."

"Shall we have a show of hands for bloody?" I asked.

"Or legs," pleaded David.

The vote was taken as Rebecca sauntered off to read a magazine, and all agreed yes, as the cause was plausible. Pretty asked for money straight away from John "£4 please. £1 Mary and £1 from Percy."

John and Percy were on the ball and responded straight away pleading their case was only £3, and nothing respectively. Pretty had other ideas, her ace in the pack.

"You both said pretty, and she is a Member of Parliament."

David joined in. "Oh, Pretty, you were good at hockey, weren't you? "

"Another £1 and yes I loved bullying-off."

The table erupted with laughter and it was noted Pretty had said pretty and owed a £1.

It soon became obvious that the idea was sound but totally unmanageable with such a motley lot. John and Percy put £40 in each. Pretty got a tenner out but the audience were amazed when David put £200 in with the calmness of a very rich man. David said he fancied a bloody Mary. You have always fancied her, my husband cajoled him.

"Only when there is a Y in the day." David's reply was consistent but with hopefulness.

Rebecca was moving around and misheard.

"Have you cut yourself, Mary, or is it the wrong time of the month?"

I scowled at her. "We were talking about your bloody Mary nails, dear." Rebecca eyed them up as she held them up. "I do love them."

I served the food on our large patio/veranda, the awning extremely useful. Pretty said a handsome man had demonstrated some Fischer heaters and she had ordered one. She was ready to tease us with her wicked sense of humour.

"Well, he got it out and I had to put my hand on it, it got so hot so quickly and lasted such a long time I just had to order one."

"But you have at least six heaters in your house," I remarked.

"Yes, seven, actually but I may want him to come back six more times with a smile and a wink." That even had Rebecca laughing.

Percy said suddenly, "Talking of seven, there has been

some trouble at the golf club, Police and locals complaining of night-time activities near the hole."

"Oh," I said, as innocently as possible. "No doubt the committee will sort it out."

"Yes, they need to as people are coming from far and wide, had to put more sanitation down and try and cordon it off. Rumour has it, it might be burnt down on bonfire night at the seventh."

Rebecca was miles away. "But that is on the fifth."

Everyone smiled except Rebecca, who gave a Goldie Hawn expression from *Rowan & Martin's Laugh-in*, for those old enough to remember. John diverted the conversation by opening the champagne. We toasted life and to a better future. My two children rang and promised to put some money in for the food bank. A surprise call from John's identical twin, Donald, in London. He sent his best wishes to all at the table and said he had asked around at work an amazing £2000. John could not thank him enough. He told us all there were 300 staff working twenty-four hours a day and he asked for a £5 a head but some gave £10 and more, so he topped it up to a round £2000.

"Must have an important job?" David enquired.

"Oh yes, civil servant had over twenty-five years and now head of a department. Very clever with computers. Might see him at Christmas."

We hardly mentioned the dreaded topic of Covid. My guests knew we were having a torrid time. John had become very irritable and depressed. We argued over the slightest and silly incidents that we had never done before. We were surviving but even I was a little disconsolate. Percy was exceptionally busy. Domestic cases in vast numbers along with our problems. He looked weary but happy the money was coming in. Pretty was fine with her work at the estate Agents and David was a man of millions. John had managed to get into work, but still not allowed in at Starling. He spent more time satisfying his creditors and using any government help for our diminishing bank balance. The council had helped by reducing the rates for a year but still the books did not balance in our favour. Rebecca had a third glass of prosecco that had replaced the champagne. She was flirting with Percy and displaying more leg than normal. As for me, I as always was the perfect hostess, so I thought, but I did like teasing David. It was a relief from the changing circumstance I had found myself in. The drinks, food and conversation flowed effortlessly towards midnight. Time to go. Percy was always the first to announce that as Rebecca became an embarrassment. Such a difference from her early demeanour. Oh, the power of drink and witty company. It was also getting cold outside despite lighting our Chimnea and candles still burning.

The next incident changed everything.

We were all about to leave the table. David as usual was drunk. He managed to slur his words towards me. "Thanks for a wonderful evening, will you sleep with me?"

I gave my standard reply. "When?"

"Only when there is a Y in the day." There was almost a chorus from the others, but they refrained from joining in, more mimicking the words silently. We all knew by now this parting offer, the problem was when he farted and we all smelt it except John, who was beginning to cough and was sweating a little.

To say it was a stampede to get out was an understatement. I was left horrified and frightened. My life was about to go full circle.

It was about six days later when he got worse and was admitted to hospital. I was tested and proved positive but given Remdesedir. I lost my husband on the 15th of August, 2020.

I hardly saw him at the end as I was also fighting for my life. He did have asthma and the stress at work apparently did not help. The nursing staff were incredible and under tremendous strain, some not having any holidays. My breathing recovered quickly, and I was one of the fortunate ones not to lose my smell. It was like being in a futuristic film, faces you could not see, names on the uniforms. I learnt eye language and yearned for that night on the patio with John. I tried not to cry but sometimes I failed. Male and female nurses of different races and cultures held my hand with gloves on. Love and help is there, but we do not always appreciate that they do this for everyone. Long live our gallant nurses and carers. I smiled as I thought of John getting the same love and care before he went on that unknown journey – the staircase to heaven.

The funeral took place on Thursday, September 10th. There were a few outside and thirty inside. I was numb with shock.

My family came up but left the next day. His twin, Donald, did the same. I felt like a prisoner in my own home. It was not till Saturday evening September 26th the five of us met again. I was a lost tearful soul and only Zoom to keep me going and the phone. I did not enjoy walking on my own, but sometimes went to a local bird sanctuary and bought items in the shop and had a drink of tea or coffee. The sounds of the birds and the simple calmness of this type of sanctuary helped me. I did not want to converse with people just yet. The church could not bring John back and if they had, was he now reincarnated and what was he? The daft things we believe or think about are a whirlwind of imagination linking hope with facts and plain logic. I was now a very worried lady and my first guest would be Percy.

Saturday, September 26th

I had not bothered to make myself look like the gorgeous hostess. The food I had prepared for this dinner party was a simple beef stew with lots of red wine. The slow cooker was called into action for the first time as the autumn chill arrived. Jacket potatoes and two vegetables with two fruit pies from the local farm shop would suffice. I knew no one would mind. My children had insisted I do it and try and get back to normality. In fact, it was them that ran or emailed my friends as they knew that I would need them. They had all responded, and John's twin was coming up especially for it. He was happily married so it was not a matchmaking move, but I was going to find it visually difficult with him in the house. In a strange way I was looking forward to seeing Donald again. I was sat putting the cards of condolence away when the doorbell went. I felt rooted to my chair and shouted come in. Percy came in on his own with two folders under his arms. As soon as he came into view, I cracked… maybe I hoped it was John.

"Why, why, why, have they taken my John? You see the numbers on the television and think it will never happen to us." I was crying as Percy walked towards his seat with sadness in his eyes, I continued. "I have just taken down all those cards, I never saw him much at the end." I took my handkerchief again to my eyes. "What will I do, where am I going? Oh, Percy, have you any good news for me?"

Percy opened both folders and with a gloomy look. "Are you ready for this?"

"Got to hear it sometime." I resigned myself to getting the facts and wiped away my tears. Have you ever had a dagger straight through your heart, then sat speechless and yet no pain?

He sighed heavily. "Nursing homes in trouble financially, one a lot worse than the other. You do not qualify for the government handout of £50,000 as he was not a carer/NHS employee, simply an owner. Death insurance does not cover acts of war and pandemics. You do not have a limited company. The house is collateral so will have to be sold. The car is leased and will have to be returned. Suppliers of specialist equipment for the Starling Nursing Home are demanding money as they too are leased. In a nutshell, Mary, you are bankrupt, even with council help on the rates. If you borrow from the government at a cheap rate it still needs repaying. With lower incomes from fewer residents not covering outgoings the business is in the red. The banks have stopped some payments as you will be aware and withdrawn your overdraft allowance. The HSBC is not always the listening bank it used to be."

"The old banger is in my name." My Renault diesel Clio

was very economical, but the big doors were a nuisance, especially trying to park and get out in confined spaces, even at Asda. I sank further in my chair.

"Have you been paid?"

Percy quickly added, with a sense of purpose and a more pleasing look, he had obtained money for me and himself. He declared that as soon as was told of John's death he had swiftly contacted the two nursing homes and demanded £2000 from each for his services, and the same to be paid for me as my wages from each account. It was fortunate that payments up to a maximum of £2000 could be authorised by each nursing home on instruction from Percy or each manageress. That had allowed us to take some extravagant and longer holidays occasionally. Percy confidently announced that would cover him for two months' work at each home. He then advised me to transfer the said money to a different bank. We went to my computer and it took less than ten minutes to do the said transfer. I was the proud owner of a Santander account with £4600, as I put what little extra I had in as well. I had hardly checked my accounts as it was too depressing watching them go down. I was silent with the shock of my situation. I went to the kitchen and stirred the beef stew in the slow cooker. Percy had gone back to his chair after helping me on the computer.

Returning to the room, I made a simple statement: "Donald is due here soon." Percy had met him at the funeral.

"Yes, I know, we have a lot to talk about before the others come. Rebecca is coming later as she's gone to get her nails done. She is deciding what new colour to change from black. Pretty is coming before David."

I did not think this was unusual for Percy to organise. He had his solicitor's hat on today, but I did not get the point of his interest in Donald. I was still in shock, listening but not planning anything except dinner. At this point, Percy said he would be back in ten minutes as he had forgotten an important document. I could tell the way Percy looked at me I needed to change. I decided to pre-empt any comments.

"Gosh, I will put my war paint on and find something a bit more glamorous, see you in ten."

Nearer fifteen minutes later, Percy came back in without knocking.

"Found the document, Donald is just parking up, seen the car."

When Donald walked in, it lifted my spirits. He had a small bag for an overnight stay. As an identical twin it was difficult not to call him John. Percy and Donald acknowledged each other with appropriate introductions. Donald hugged me and apologised.

"Sorry for not staying longer after the funeral I had important work to do."

"You were wonderful at working out John's passwords for me, twin instinct? I would have been lost without that help."

"Mixture of that and my work colleagues, anyway, how are you coping, Mary?"

"All bad news, I am not sure how to tell the children, they certainly do not want Grandma full time".

"Is it that bad?" Donald looking agonizingly at Percy; the folders on view. I wiped tears from my eyes as Percy continued. "Worse than bad, I'm afraid, I am going to ask Pretty to put the house on the market."

There are moments when you think you can have no more shocks in life but how wrong was I? It was Donald who took over the stage after he had been upstairs. A quick wash and shave he returned ready for the evening. Mugs of tea prepared as it was now nearing 5pm.

"Mary, it is time to come clean with you." I wondered what the hell he was going to say. "Without John, Percy and your delightful teasing of David we would never be in such a strong position at work. I am not a simple pen pusher at the civil service. I am a cyber expert and collaborator for catching criminals/gangs scamming the government. We also help other countries, hence the size of our workforce. By inviting a con man here, an excellent one we must admit, we secretly recorded his comments. That way he inadvertently gave us a great insight into how the criminal mind works. Any information is better than none."

"Where the hell did you hide the recorder?"

Percy now looked like a dog with a bone full of meat. "I or John put it under the table where he always sat, the table cover hid it."

"Bloody hell, you were in on this as well?" I was astonished. Donald opened his own folder. "This is why we had to meet before the others came and discuss the next problem. Over twenty years of experience in this field, I am now the chief negotiator to recuperate as much money as possible for the government that has been paid out in scams or mistakenly to companies. The PPE market is worth billions and early panic led to mistakes. If we can recall a minimum of 70% depending on the amount without court cases, complications, embarrassments that is regarded as a good deal."

At this stage I interrupted. "It pays to be a good con man/scammer." As I said the words the penny dropped "DAVID!" Percy and Donald opened their respective files. It was Percy now with his judge's hat on that explained.

"He started two companies in Turkey when he went back in March. He found a few women to make some PPE in Bodrum. The specification had been given him by Pretty as John had asked his secretary to email her. Pretty could make a few for the Starling Home but not thousands that David was promising. He brought back good samples. The scam offices in Ankara said 200,000 masks would be sent as well as 10,000 gowns. One company was charging a lot more as it seemed the quality was better. However, to get this shipment they needed cash up front. The other company was based elsewhere so it did not seem obvious with two different addresses. Because the amounts of money were under three million per company it was pay and hope. He even had the audacity to say that due to demand they had an extra 100,000 face masks and 3000 gowns that were waiting to go to another country, but they had not come up with the money. Pay now and it will be diverted to the UK and their order will be sent later. The government had new inexperienced members in the

Cabinet and important positions. They were under pressure from the media. An element of panic buying. It was a bit like the speaker of the House of Commons – *order-order-order*. Now we are trying to get some money back. The goods simply never arrived."

It was Donald's turn to complete the plan. "Mary, we have all the evidence to put him away for a long time and get back most of the money. However, if we do a deal with David and say get back 90% and then Percy pays me 70% there is a tidy bit to share between the three of us."

"Is this legal?"

The two of them simply looked at each other and Percy said convincingly, "This is business and commission only for my services so very legal."

"How do we get David to hand you so much money back?"

Donald was quick to reply. "The threat of prison, lots of Covid in jail, he is bound to agree, job's a good un, no problem, been there once will not want to go back."

"So why do you want me, you have all the aces?"

It was Percy's turn to respond to my question. "But you are the Queen of Hearts, every little persuasion is better."

"So how much are we talking about?"

Donald checked his notes. "Four million pounds near as damn it. We will clear a cool £100,000 each – minimum, depending on the agreement. If we get back 90% it is over £200,000 each with 70% for the government. We ask for it all back first. We have the evidence and all the aces."

I had no idea how to react. It sounded plausible but also

illegal. I was virtually penniless, no future and depressed. "Okay. I agree, the money is a good incentive."

Donald finished off the meeting as the doorbell rang.

"Be not too greedy and no one will investigate further, we will call ourselves the three Masketeers."

We laughed and held our hands up as per the tradition. It was Pretty that had arrived. I introduced her to Donald. She exchanged a sorrowful hello with me. The camera gave it away.

"I will start in the house. Need to take photos and have the house on the market within seven days. Percy told me you will be moving, a brighter new carpet in the entrance," Pretty politely observed.

We went back to view the worn small entrance carpet. David and Rebecca arrived as I told them all that I will be moving between Basingstoke and Wimbledon. I sighed as I mentioned to be near my children and grandchildren. I shuddered as I looked at David and wondered about what would happen soon. My mind was in no fit state as I mumbled, "May have to rent and go back nursing, Pretty, will you please look at my options near Basingstoke, I cannot afford to be in Wimbledon."

Rebecca and David were suitably remorseful towards me. Although they arrived together it was pure coincidence. It was now early evening and it started with a storm before the tsunami. Rebecca was showing off her nails, blowing them as they still smelt fresh and wet, and mask in the NHS colours. An outfit, outrageously colourful, that put Pretty's outfit and mine well in the shade. David instinctively put his size 10 feet into the party.

"Bet your nails get more blow jobs than Percy."

Her reaction was full of hope and intent. "You should be hung, drawn and quartered."

Percy, forever the arbitrator, joined in. "No good to me I need my clients to live, repeat offenders means more money. I am not sure such a comment is suitable," he said as he looked at Donald and me.

"Sorry, Mary, could not resist. Nice to meet you, Donald, at last, gosh you are just like John."

"David the con man I presume." Donald's response was akin to Doctor Livingstone. "Rumours, only rumours, you must differ in some way as identical twins."

"Actually, I was the younger and half an inch smaller, but you can hardly tell."

At this point, I decided it was time to kill two birds with one stone. I had found David's comment about Rebecca's nails rather funny and I had to get David's attention. This sudden change in conversation gave me the perfect opportunity. I looked more longingly than usual at David before I set the tone for the evening.

"Size does matter."

I remember them all laughing. Pretty was quick to spot my eye movement and gazumped me. She caressed David's leg, "Shall I adjudicate?"

David got up nearly as fast as Pretty put her hand on his leg. He moved towards the drinks table admiring me before uttering, "Well, that helps my cause, Mary, I have a sizeable pocket as well as—"

"Patience is a virtue that you clearly do not have, David," Percy said.

Rebecca confirmed her thoughts "You are a wretched con man and seducer of women. Bring back the middle ages and four good shire horses to pull you apart."

I noticed the men wincing at the thought. Pretty was quick to add, "What about me?" as she hoped David would pay more attention to her. Percy was now in the chairman role.

"Fill your glasses, time for business. Donald, please introduce yourself and your role at work."

The strange thing about having a secret recorder is that the results are astonishingly accurate. Donald did focus his eyes on David while he began his introduction. This caused him to be uneasy in his chair.

"I have 300 staff working on rotas 24/7 365 days of the year. You may know I work for the civil service. I am now responsible for recovering monies from individuals/companies who evade tax, scam or acquire money through illegal means. It is hard intensive work. We are successful otherwise we would not have 300 employed. We occasionally have a good laugh in a serious environment.

We have one elderly gentleman nicknamed four eyes. He spends so much time scouring newspapers and the small print to help our cause. Then it is in front of a computer, his eyesight is terrible. At one meeting he proudly proclaimed he was on the trail of a Doctor One. He thought he might be Chinese and was Doctor Won. He or she was responsible for supplying drugs to several prisons. We allowed him to work two days on the case before a colleague told him the headline in some local paper was a misprint. It read DrOne where a capital had been put in by mistake. The headline should have read Drone takes drugs into prison."

Muffled laughter was replaced by even more as he continued his story about a warehouse at a dock had been raided and 20,000 clown outfits were seized. Lost in translation, he said, should have been 20,000 gowns for the NHS. I gave my best Chinese accent. "Why you make silly mistake?"

Rebecca piped up, "Lost in Translation will win next year at Cheltenham." Apparently, it was a good horse.

Laughter eased the strain of what was to follow. Glasses were replenished as I checked the stew. I decided to allow them all to eat the main course first. It was tense and the conversation varied from the coming American election, *Strictly* on television, a bit about football and Brexit. We girls mentioned *Bake-off* and other food programmes as we finished the stew that was welcomed and enjoyed by all. I was pleased to take the plates away. Prosecco for Rebecca after her orange juice, three red wines and two beers, Percy was ready to take the chair.

"As you all know, Mary has her own problems, but David you have even more serious worries."

Percy and Donald each opened their respective folders as Percy continued. "Donald has produced this evidence that you are guilty of acquiring vast sums of money, not supplying said goods and scamming the government of millions."

Pretty gasped but surprisingly looked at David with more affection, pleased that someone had taken the government for a ride as they had done to her parents. The Windrush scandal was still news. She offered him a walk in the garden. It was Rebecca who could not wait. "Hang him high."

Donald triumphantly said, "Four million in these bank accounts, prison for you, but we may have a way out."

David was remarkably calm. I was beginning to admire him.

"I will take prison. They treat me like a god there. I am no killer, child abuser, drug pusher or rapist. I am respected in prison. I have no reason to stay here. Mary is leaving and Covid may or may not get me. I do not care. Her Majesty's Government will feed me with a roof over my head. I will come out in a few years' time. I will have most of that money. In the words of that famous Clint Eastwood film, I am Bad, Mary is Good, but you, Donald, are Ugly."

Donald angrily retorted, "Ugly in actions but not in looks. I can have you arrested within the hour, your accounts frozen now and the money transferred. Bail will be high and prison definite. Second offenders get a longer sentence."

"So why have you not done it? I am no fool, I suggest you check those accounts properly. The trail is not as easy as you think. You did say there was a way out. In prison you learn that deals are done. Come on, Pretty, I will take up on that offer and go in the garden while they ponder. I enjoyed cell number 44 by the way."

Donald and Percy looked as though they had been knocked down in a boxing match. Was it the wine or plain survival instinct but I began to smell money and a better life?

"You need me more than you thought," I looked at Percy, "your rates are extortionate; I want free conveyancing for my move down south and 80% of the profit if I keep him out of prison and get a deal."

"No way" was the joint response.

When a woman gives a certain look, the message is clearer than talking. They moved to a corner for a quick conflab and came back with 50%. I was enjoying my new position of power. "You expect me to surrender to a scoundrel for the cause and only 50%. You both have jobs and good income, I need 80%." I was becoming excited, a complete distraction from my recent loss.

Rebecca had her say. "Marry the bastard, poison him and keep all the money."

After a swift chat, they came back to me and said they needed 15% each and would give me free solicitors' fees for six months. I drank some more red wine slowly. I was not good at maths, but it sounded okay, so I accepted. I had more than doubled my share, I now had the hard job of seducing David into a deal. Pretty and David returned. Percy and Donald were looking at the files and simply acknowledged David's look and mumbled to him, "Talk later." Rebecca and Pretty went to look at a magazine, I took David's arm and escorted him back into the garden with our glasses refilled. David had no idea what I was up to and why.

We went to the gazebo. He enquired what deal they were talking about. I pretended I had no idea but thought I heard they would be happy if they got 90% back. I preferred to lower my guard and open an extra button. Our legs mingled slightly and used the drink as an excuse. I bravely went straight to the point.

"Do you really want to go to prison at your age when I am available?"

David seemed convinced enough, especially after a short peck on his cheeks. His next comment shook me. "Two million pounds and would you sleep with me when there is a Y in the day?"

"No good to me if you are in prison. Money seems no object to you. I will give it serious thought, but not interested in marriage."

I really had no idea how far to go with him. I did not want to sleep with anyone just yet, and I was engulfed in unknown territory. The night air was cool, so we returned to the table to have the sweet course. A knife could have cut the atmosphere, virtually no conversation. It was the classic spaghetti western scenario of eyes looking at eyes, weighing up who was real or bluffing. My time in hospital gave me an advantage. Pound signs everywhere but who would get what or any? I played the classic film score of the late Ennio Morricone, *Ecstasy of Gold*. It was the perfect backdrop to the situation.

It was Percy who broke the silence. "Not many golfers at the funeral."

And it was Pretty that returned her verdict. "Perhaps they were under par." At least it raised a restrained laugh, but the atmosphere was still strained.

I decided to ring my children. Well wishes to each other

and I told them I did not want to know about *Strictly* as I has recorded it. Told them I was going to be looking to move down there hopefully by Christmas. Rebecca stuck with the prosecco while Pretty and I had coffee. The three men retired to a corner to discuss the deal to stop David going to jail. I took Pretty's chocolates around and gave a subtle nod to Donald and Percy when David was not looking. I hoped David was still keen on me. There was a bit of swearing in the corner and defiance from David. We looked at clothes magazines. I hoped I could afford some soon. It felt like Brexit in the corner and it finished with David saying he would come round in the morning and let David know before he left for London. I did not care about the deal as whatever will be will be. Donald retired to his room as he needed to use his iPad and contact London. Percy, Rebecca and Pretty also went and David surprisingly asked to stay for a coffee. We were alone perhaps for the first time ever. I tentatively asked, "Is the two million still on the table?"

"I meant to say £2000, silly of me."

I remember getting annoyed. "What do you take me for?"

"That has already been decided, we are now haggling over the price, surely I deserve to inspect the goods."

He did try to fondle me, but I managed to satisfy him with a cuddle and a kiss. I was pleased Donald was upstairs even though I did feel safe and happy with David. A funny easy-going con man is better than a drunken idiot. I escorted him to the door and like an obedient dog he went home. It was then that I trusted him and felt a glow for what the future might hold. I passed Donald's room on the way to bed and said goodnight to each other, not knowing any deal details. It was the men who irritably needed to be the decision makers.

It was 9.30am when David rang the doorbell the next morning. Donald was deliberately on his iPad to London upstairs. David was straight to the point, a bit like Percy.

"If we agree a figure it will have to go to a solicitor. I will have to buy a house near you, or pay for an extension on an existing property, if we are not to be married. The contract with the word sleep that I have used will be replaced by sex on a regular basis. I want no loopholes. Witnesses, legal and the offer is a straight one million pounds. I need to know now if you accept, then I will consider Donald's offer."

I was dressed in casual but smart attire. I tried to stop my nerves of excitement showing. I hoped it was a genuine offer. He suddenly became more attractive by the pound. I thought for a while as I sat down, weak at the knees. Was I an expensive whore or did I really want him? I gave an answer, but I did not know where it came from.

"Fourteen-day cooling-off period. I want to see my children at Christmas. The deal will start on January 1st, 2021. I will be your New Year's present."

I had surrendered. The white flag was clear above my head. He would explore me, and I knew what arranged marriages might be like now I had decided. But would I enjoy him? I was shaking with nerves or was it excitement. David concluded he would get Percy to sort out a contract. Donald appeared and exchanged a good morning to David.

I went to the kitchen and left them to talk. I heard conversations on the mobile phones with Percy, who was in his office. Donald came in to say goodbye and left for London. David was smiling with a mischievous look. I felt his eyes undress me, which I had got used to, but he did not stay. His parting words, "Deal's done, see you in November for the draught copies to view. Donald is coming up then. Final agreement by December 8th to give the fourteen-day cooling-off period and all monies paid before Christmas."

I said nothing but was annoyed no one had told me the full picture. How much was I going to get with this government deal? Percy and Donald had not told me. I now had to wait till November as when I asked, they simply said it all had to be ratified but no figures given to me. I kept my cool but underneath I felt excluded and a little angry and very suspicious.

Early November

Before our scheduled business/dinner party meeting for Saturday, November 7th, I had to take one final walk on my own to the seventh hole before the obelisk was burnt down. It was a good thing I went in early October before the new lockdowns started. There were some golfers, but they did not see me take a chisel to mark our names on it. I found a spot next to Z&C and put in M&J. There were so many now who had admitted what they might have done or not as the case may be. I did read the poem and was pleased the extra two verses were on view. The telescope had been repaired. It had been on television at the *Repair Shop*. I must have missed that programme, but a video was on sale in the clubhouse with the presentation including several members who were present. It only needed a sixpence to use, but they charged 50p for one, three for a £1 and twenty for a fiver. All profits to the club. I bought the video and £1 for three tanners as we remember them. It was a lovely walk to the seventh hole. I held my hand out but there was no one to hold it. I did not stay too long this time. I used all three tanners and spotted some poor shots. I wondered who Big Boy from Barnsley was. That was inscribed near the telescope with a mobile number that was unrecognizable. At least it made me smile before I cried.

The police and the committee decided in the interest of public safety and decency it would be burnt on bonfire night or the first available date when fires were allowed afterwards. The poem was to be saved and put in the clubhouse or near the seventh hole. The telescope would be found a suitable spot. Decisions on that might be made at the next Zoom meeting. The treasurer wanted it to stay as there had been a huge increase in enquiries for membership. Due to the pandemic no new members were being accepted. As far as I was concerned, it was a pity that too many people knew about it with all the modern communication tools. Ignorance is bliss I thought.

The committee were still wondering if the late Sean Connery, whose ashes were to be spread on the old course of St Andrew's in Scotland, had signed and returned a memento before he died. He had played at the course many years earlier when the club raised money for charity. Members paid £200 a head for a round of golf with several celebrities. Dinner and speeches had made it a day and night to remember that was often recalled at the bar.

Connery had played a particularly good shot at the now famous seventh, tapping in for a two. The committee had contacted his agent saying they would now rename the seventh to '007' and place a placard next to it with an inscription "You only live twice" with his name and room for his signature. Twice had a line through it and replaced with "once". They had sent the poem and reminded him of his great shot and his picture that hung in the clubhouse with all participants plus one of him on his own. It had been sent before the pandemic and his death on the 31st of October in Nassau. They were waiting fingers crossed it had been signed and in the post.

Time to move on as I was spotted by a cricketer leaving the golf club. "Sorry to hear about your husband, MCC."

I had not seen him for ages and I wondered if I was doing the right thing with David. I would find a cricket club down south and continue doing teas if required; I found it rewarding and a lovely hobby. I had been unable to do teas when the short season restarted due to my situation and the law that players and officials brought their own food.

We all met in a sombre mood as another lockdown threatened us all. DN postcode goes all the way from near Barnsley/Doncaster to Cleethorpes. I was in a lower tier than south and west Yorkshire, being officially in Lincolnshire so the meeting was not only for business but legal. We were all sat together; the two tables meant we were well apart. I often wondered how lucky my guests back in July were not to get Covid. Good job we were outside that night John got the virus symptoms. I did open a window and it was surprisingly warm for November. Donald was staying the night and did the drinks. He insisted on a Thai takeaway that was due later as his contribution. We all sat wondering exactly what agreements had been reached. It is all in the detail.

It was Pretty who started the conversation that night…

"Had some interest in the house, but viewings may have to wait a while. I have found some rentable ones nearer Basingstoke. One of the ones you liked has been sold and I put an offer in for the other subject to raising of funds. Some agents will not allow viewings unless the money is available immediately, so Zoom only for those."

Bit of a pain but sales amazingly going through. You cannot enquire on your neighbours like that, I would never buy blind so to speak. I like to check it visually all around the area and ask questions with local people.

There were nods of approval. But she continued. "You are allowed to travel and stay overnight in a Travelodge if you are viewing properties, might be useful in the near future."

One of the children rang before *Strictly* started, I was recording as usual. I confirmed I still loved them and would be moving down there soon. Told them renting made more sense to begin with and then buy later. Percy waited for me to finish and then announced the meeting would start.

He began by saying, "This is the document drawn up between the Department of Justice v David Jones of such and such address…" It was a smaller document than the one he had for David and me. It simply said in return for a payment of 3.4 million pounds no further action will be taken against the said David Jones. This was in relation to goods ordered and not supplied but paid for in advance for the said goods but never received. There were lots of other legal jargon, but I could now work out my percentage. My maths had improved rapidly when it affected me. Luckily, the figures were easy to work out. I would get a share of 1.2 million less what they had agreed David to keep. 70% of 4 million = 2.8 the sum in the agreement leaving 600,000 to share x 70% = 420,000 for me. David quietly read the contracts very carefully. I was drunk with happiness at the thought of all that money as a bonus. I wondered how they would change that figure for the government, but I did not care. They pointed to where David had to sign and then space for the two witnesses in this case Pretty and me. David said he would only sign when our contract was signed as well.

The next contract had been done by Rebecca on Percy's behalf. The full-time secretary had not been used for these. Names, current addresses and dates of birth clearly printed. The draft agreement clearly stating 1 million to be paid to solicitors Percy Dickinson by December 8th and paid to Mary after the fourteen-day cooling-off period on December 22nd, 2020. Mary allowed to visit her children over Christmas and the contract to formally begin on January 1st, 2021. Rebecca had deliberately put sleep in the contract."

"Replace that with sex or no deal," David was adamant.

At this point I nudged David's leg and said, "Okay, but only when there is a Y in the day, after all it has been your catch phrase for years."

Everyone laughed and David saw the joke. Rebecca changed the word to sex followed by the phrase only when there is a Y in the day. We all initialled the changes and signed the draft agreement. Percy reminded us all that it would only be legal when the agreed contracts are finally signed. A draft agreement is not a final agreement even if signed. I was not duly worried by such technicalities. Donald produced his government draft document and we all signed again. I really could not believe what was happening. The champagne opened and toasts all around. Percy reminded us all that we had to meet on December 8th to confirm the said monies had been paid into his account. New documents would be signed again with the alterations.

I put on the television as the health secretary Mr Hancock was making a speech about the impending lockdown tiers. The media had attacked him unfairly I thought. These politicians were damned if they did and damned if they did not.

Rebecca again delighted us all by proclaiming, "My dad says it only lasts half an hour."

"That is Hancock's half hour from years ago, stupid woman."

David was on form, but Rebecca had the final word. "Bet you cannot last half an hour, Percy, am I worth a million?"

"Yes, darling, and muttered BAHT."

The conversation drifted to Bitcoin and if David was involved. "Not a chance," he said, "great idea though, someone is making millions." The American election took centre stage, more champagne and Rebecca was revealing toenails now and plenty of leg. Cue for Percy to take her home and then Pretty left, disappointed she had not captured David. She had lost some of her sparkle but was engrossed in her job and earning some money as business was brisk. Donald stopped up till I allowed David a quick grope and a snog before he left.

"You have done well out of these deals haven't you, Mary."

"Of course, look what I have to put up with for the rest of my life."

"But you do have over a million reasons for doing it," Donald concluded sarcastically and with a hint of jealousy.

On that note we retired to our own beds and he left early the next morning. December 8th would, by coincidence, be a pivotal day in the fight against Covid. I agreed with Pretty to rent a property on a three-month short-term agreement near Hook from December. I explained it gave me time to view any houses. From December 22nd, I would have enough money to buy one outright and not need to work if the right house came on the market. I felt happier and David was certainly an interesting rogue with some good points. The upfront rent cost me nearly £2000. My savings were now down below £1000. I was hopeful all would go as planned. What could possibly go wrong?

Tuesday, December 8th

For me this was the most important day since I lost my husband.

All the talk and alleged deals now had to be witnessed and signed. The lockdown with Tiers 1, 2 and 3 were confusing but necessary. Professor Witty had become a national icon. Van Tam was not far behind him. Bungling Boris took the advice of Sage. I thought sage meant intelligence, but nobody seemed to have a sensible solution. If the world was in chaos what chance had poor Boris? The opposition and the public had the answers, of course, but putting it into practice and succeeding with any solution seemed impossible. It was stay safe and try and survive. Common sense which was no longer in the dictionary was replaced by the media asking ridiculous questions and becoming more unpopular by the day. I never saw an interviewer say well done to any politician on any side of the house. They always looked for an argument to do what? Show how clever they were for bringing up another contentious subject, knowing full well they and nobody else had a truthful answer. Marcus Rashford of Manchester United football club championed the right for schoolchildren to have free meals. Was he right wing or left wing? Who cared, they deserved free meals and will he be champion again, not according to rivals Manchester City and Liverpool.

Sportsman had taken the knee for BLM (Black Lives Matter) when common sense suggests as the Good Lord would concur ALM (All Lives Matter). I was not going to get involved in these arguments as they were already in the public domain. My job was to look after number one. I watched less television. *Strictly* was my number one choice. I got honesty, affection in bucket loads and the feel-good factor was contagious. At this stage I thought Harvey (HRVY) was going to win. A bottle of wine and a nice dinner on a tray, eyes glued on a Saturday night was my pleasure. I recorded the series as I knew I could return anytime for my medicine. I gave myself ten for my indulgent spirit of pure clean enjoyment. Mary Whitehouse would have objected to the short skirts and revealing dresses so why would she watch? Maybe the tight trousers! Rock on, Bill Bailey, he is probably the only one who remembered her. Then there was the hapless Jamie who, to be fair, grew on me for his excitable manner and pure enthusiasm. Would I do the same for David?

Donald had driven up in awful foggy conditions. The rest had walked in their winter clothes. Rebecca had her nails looking like snowflakes. Percy reminded everyone that this was a perfectly legitimate business meeting, technically three bubbles in a Tier 2 area, just had to keep apart. Strangely, the atmosphere was incredibly upbeat. The vaccine had been approved some weeks before and the first two to be injected had received national stardom. Margaret Keening was the first woman to receive the vaccine in Coventry. Ironically, it was the second name that will remain in most people's memory. That was William Shakespeare who came from Stratford-upon-Avon. My learned friends at this meeting did not disappoint. They all wanted to talk about it – the air of optimism was infectious. We all tried to work out what month we might get it. Eventually it was David who got the show on the road.

"I hear William Shakespeare is going to have his second injection on the twelfth night."

Percy fell for it. "I do believe it is twenty-one days after the first."

Donald laughed loudly and joined in. "Better a witty fool, than a foolish wit."

Rebecca dived in, "But, Professor Witty is no fool."

David listened and proudly stated with an air of contemptuous authority, "Some are born great, others achieve greatness."

I advanced my thoughts to him with the flickering of my eyebrows. "How does he love me?"

Pretty surprised us all with her knowledge of Shakespeare. "With adoration, with fetish tears, with groans that thunder love, with sighs of fire."

David responded looking straight at me. "Does thou think, because thou art virtuous, there shall be no more cakes and ales."

Rebecca, not having done Shakespeare completely, had us in stitches by finishing off the subject matter, "Many a good hanging prevents a bad marriage."

Percy brought us back to our senses by helping Donald distribute six flutes of champagne. It was earlier than usual for Rebecca, but she accepted. The first toast was to the vaccine and Oxford. The second to Margaret Keening. The third to William Shakespeare. Everyone was in a good mood. I felt confident all was well. Pretty told us she had reduced the price for my house. Now we had four viewings and a sale looked likely. David instructed her to put his house on the market in the New Year. He said he would look for a house wherever I had mine. The recent lockdown had been different, poorer depressing weather, little gardening and Christmas would not be the same with most ageing parents left on their own for safety reasons. The Dickinsons had brought two bottles of champagne this time. Rebecca had done her shopping online, using Black Friday to get a discount on her favourite champagne. She was on form already on her third glass. No one seemed to care, it was as if a weight was off everyone's' shoulders. I brought over some mince pies as the takeaway was due later. Pretty was keen to tell us something.

"Well, there were about thirty of us, all crying but we were two metres apart."

Rebecca seemed to be half listening. "Whose funeral?"

"Nobody's, we were just queuing to pay at Debenhams."

Donald was philosophical. "Only the top shops will survive."

Rebecca quickly added, “Even they have gone.”

At this point Percy, with a resigned look at her, “Rebecca, do you ever pay attention?”

David had been quiet for a while, and it worried me. Percy opened the two contracts. One between the government and David and the other between ourselves. Rebecca was annoyed that she had to change the word sleep to sex but had left in “only when there is a Y in the day.”

“Do you get any days off?” she asked, as Pretty nodded in agreement.

I pre-empted any problem. “Do you think a man of his age can recover so quickly to match me?” I taunted him. “Cannot wait to find out in the New Year.”

“Blimey, you do have a dark side,” Pretty commented with a hint of admiration and jealousy. I had David exactly where I wanted him, with a wink in my eye and the ladies acknowledging my dominant style, I continued. “I might have to whip him into shape if he fails in his duty.”

Reliable Rebecca sailed into action. “Nelson expected everyone to do his duty, if not you will be hung drawn and quartered or flogged to death.” A wicked smile came over her, but David was up to it.

“What a way to go at the hands of Mary the Barbarian”.

Percy was not impressed. He wanted the business finishing. He showed David the contracts, sign here and here he explained. There was a deadly silence. David looked around at all of us.

“No deal.”

My heart sank. I had no money left and my dreams were

shattered. I tried not to show it. My shaking hands tried to hold the flute of champagne. Pretty just sat there, hopeful he might fancy her. David continued.

"You think you caught me eh? I knew about the microphones. I do have millions, but I had to think of a plan to get Mary for myself. You learn a lot in prison. I knew about your deals before you even came down, Donald. When I dropped my napkin and messed around under the table, I could see more than table legs. There it was – your microphone. I have known for years. I gave you accounts but they only had minimal amounts in. My banks are good at putting false numbers down. They get well paid for misinformation; the expression now is fake news. The good news for you guys is that I am tired of running and money does not bring total happiness. I am prepared to go to prison but the deal is £3 million not £3.4. It will not take you long to reprint those details. You still get some commission and I get Mary for the £1 million I made. If Mary is in on your plot, I respect her even more. The less she gets the better my chances for my offer and not using her fourteen-day cooling-off option to cancel."

Seeing Donald and Percy gobsmacked was becoming a habit. I aimed my reply directly at David. "The only plot I know about is you three and my garden." I was nervous and lied but tried not to show it.

Rebecca who does not normally pay attention broke the tension.

"You filthy rich—" but Pretty continued, "—clever bastard, pity you do not fancy me."

It was too cold to go outside and the food had arrived. There was an uneasy silence, but David got his cheque book out. He wrote out two cheques. Both to Percy Dickinson, one for £3 million and another for £1 million. He had a swagger to him that I found seductive. I had never seen such large amounts of money on two cheques and even Pretty was in awe.

"I sign these when the new contracts are in front of me signed by all here."

I realised I had to pretend I knew nothing about the deal with the government. I adoringly looked at Percy and Donald playing the forlorn woman. "It is my future please can you do the deal?"

I knew we were taking a big hit on our commission, but I still had some to play around with.

"Shall we go upstairs and reprint the deal?" I asked them both as I realised this was the only way for the three of us to get together and agree our own dividend if Donald accepted the new proposal. Rebecca and Pretty went to the kitchen to get the plates and uncover the Thai food so people could help themselves. David sat in his chair sipping the champagne like a rogue film producer. I knew they would want me to take less than 70% as the dividend had just dropped £400,000. The old deal gave them £90,000 each and me a massive £420,000. I felt like crying. This was a mess. I feared a jail sentence and worse still – no deal. There was only £200,000 left in the pot as Donald pointed out. After a brief chat they offered a third each, the original idea. I was snookered. I reminded Percy about the six months free solicitors' fees and could they stretch to £80,000 for me. I was trapped as they had seen the £1 million cheque. Percy resolved it, forever the judge. One year's solicitors' fees and £70,000 for me. They would get £65,000 each. "Owt is better than nowt," he exclaimed as any Yorkshireman would concur.

We ate the food while the new contracts were printed out automatically. I would have to go back to work, as house prices were exorbitant down south. I would not want to rent for ever. David was looking at the apartment I had paid to rent and other houses in the area. Pretty was very efficient and I liked her a lot. She concluded her assessment.

"Paying seven hundred a month for a one-bed is not better than buying for under 500,000 for a three-bed semi near Hook."

My maths brain said at least £500,000 in the bank and maybe a lady of leisure. Wimbledon was a nonstarter as all my money would disappear if I bought. Hence the reason Elizabeth and Charlie only rented. The Thai food was delicious. Cooked in giant woks in open view and then either eaten on simple tables or delivered, this was a popular local inexpensive restaurant. Red and Green curries with vegetables and some fish dishes, it was a feast Donald had ordered but insisted David paid for. David surprisingly had paid for it when it was delivered while we were upstairs. According to Pretty he gave the driver a nice tip as well. It was beginning to feel a bit like Brexit, not Christmas. Would the deal now be signed, and I get my money on the 22nd, after the fourteen-day cooling-off period. I was in my best glad rags as some ladies put it. David eyed me up and my defences had been smashed away by his dirty money. I did not care now I only thought of my move and being near my family. The papers duly appeared. It was Rebecca's turn to read out the fine print. She did it remarkably well considering her flute was never empty. She paid particular attention to the altered text that David had noticed at the previous meeting.

"No marriage for now and sex only when there is a Y in the day." It did raise yet another laugh and lots of winks from them all except Donald who only wanted his deal sorted. I finished off my champagne with relief after David signed all the documents. Everyone followed where instructed as Percy then refilled the glasses. A final toast was made by Donald; he raised his glass and pointed it at David. "To the finest con man I have met." I realised then why he and Percy respected him.

Rebecca refused to join in but muttered, "Hang him with the finest rope possible." I knew she meant the slimmest rather than best, but the message was clear. The phone went and my granddaughter asked if Santa was having the vaccine. I relayed the question to my guests for help. I was inspired. "I will go and check Santa's website."

I let Pretty talk to her for a while.

"Just found out he and the reindeer have had the first dose a few days ago as part of the test programme. The good news is that on Christmas Eve he is stopping at Oxford for the second doses. Put your mother on. Yes, coming for Christmas but need to be back for the 27/28th. I think we are all meeting for one final time to check all monies have cleared and in respective bank accounts. Bye. Love you all. Just a reminder I can use my flat now if Covid restrictions worsen, bye".

Percy, to my relief, said he and Pretty had done the paperwork and I could now use the one-bed flat from Monday the 14th. David was smirking and I knew what was going through his mind. I told him it was only a short-term rent, and it was a double bed. "January 1st is when all your birthdays come at once."

I was in a happy teasing mood. I felt ready for him. Rebecca was admiring her toenails now as snow fell outside. Rebecca and Pretty felt gazumped and annoyed at David. I asked if Donald was coming back for the 27/28th meeting.

"No reason why not. There are a few loose ends to tie up. I have another call up north to make so should be no problem, weather permitting".

"Can you do me a big favour and pick me up on the 23rd and then bring me back, save driving my old banger?"

Donald did not look happy but succumbed. "If no one else can, yes."

David was swiftly on his metal. "No problem I will take you down, meet the family and you can bring her back."

It was nice to have two men fighting over me in two far better cars. Donald had a big Mercedes, but David had a BMW. I did not care what was under the bonnet they were warm and comfortable. It seemed a good plan as I could get a lift to north London, where Donald lived when I returned.

I was going to be well-off and have a new lover. I did not dare count my chickens after recent events but was confident all was now well. The evening was fizzling out as snow continued falling. Christmas like no other was just around the corner. The strain of the deals was taking its toll on everyone. They all left in an orderly fashion.

Pretty teased David as they left so I could hear. "Why not sleep with me when there is a Y in the day till January 1st?"

David came back to kiss me again goodnight. "I only have eyes for you."

Donald left the next morning. I now had to wait till the next big day December 27th or 28th to be decided by Percy. We were working on the coronavirus travel allowance days.

Tuesday, December 29th

The final meeting had to be December 29th to make sure the monies had reached all the accounts as the 28th was a Bank Holiday. The new strain of coronavirus had caused more disruption. More U-turns than on the roads. Mariah Carey had been Christmas number 1 and Downing Street had advertised albums and CDs from Tears for Fears for sale. The wit of the British public on song. The meeting for all six of us was scheduled for 1pm rather than a formal dinner party or similar. This was in case the banks had to be contacted or estate agents as events were unfolding. I was ecstatic as the 1 million had been in my account since the 23rd. I had been extra generous with my cheques to my children and grandchildren which they gleefully took from the Christmas tree, the surprise in colourful envelopes. We all met at the house near Farnham as that was Tier 2. The Waverley district had avoided a Tier 3 or 4 much to my relief. They had met David when he brought me down like a dutiful lamb following his mother. It is amazing how family can suddenly find good in a wealthy person and to keep me in a good mood. I was happier with David when we travelled. He liked the Classic FM and we switched to local channels occasionally to check the traffic. Good thing we did, as we avoided a long delay. He was the pure gentleman, different from his social behaviour that we were accustomed to at parties. Opening doors for me, being polite and no rude jokes with my family. Gave several full bottles of quality wine out. He only stayed for lunch, no alcohol and then left as per our agreement. He had even bought presents wrapped up for my grandchildren as well as one for me. I felt sorry for him and another awful drive back north. As per the story there was no room at the inn, but he seemed so happy to wait for me. I let him openly cuddle and kiss me. He even got me under the mistletoe, much to the amusement of my grandchildren. I was warming to him more than I had done before. I wondered what he would think of my new book I had got him for Christmas. It was titled *50 places to visit around Basingstoke*. By the time Mathew drove me to Donald's house on the 28th I felt nervous about the next meeting. Time was running out. I was under contract to David. My life was about to change forever. I asked for understanding from John who I had secretly spoken to since he died. I smiled and cried often when alone with his ghost. The daft things we think when we have endured a close loss. I just thought of the Beatles song 'Life goes on oh bla di, oh bla da' and kept repeating the line.

We arrived early evening on the Sunday. We ate, had non-alcoholic drinks and retired early. Donald still checking what had happened at work.

We all met at 1pm the following day.

It was Percy who chaired the meeting. "Welcome all, hope you had as good a Christmas as possible." We all joined in with the response "Like no other." Percy continued, "All monies paid to me by David cleared. The agreed amounts sent to Donald's office and Mary's accounts." Donald and I nodded, smiled and confirmed softly that the monies had indeed been paid from Percy's account. Donald's had only arrived in his account today. I was a regular client, and the transfer was duly quicker as we both used Santander. Pretty looked extremely happy. Her smile lit up the room as she announced the house had been sold. I had known for a week but had told no one till the money had been paid to Percy as my acting solicitor. There were boxes in the lounge and another room filled with some household goods. As part of the deal, I had included most contents and increased that value. The house sale went to the mortgage company and other debts, but I kept the contents money. A better deal for me. Percy had agreed to give Pretty a bonus for the house sale and David had given her a Christmas cheque. Pretty was not interested in our deals but was pleased with the announcement of more Windrush money being available. I had to lighten the mood and tease David. I thanked him for my Christmas presents, a red-letter afternoon tea day for two, as well as a Spa day for two at Champneys. Time for action.

"I am going to my flat soon, how about paying half my rent?" I could have guessed his reply.

"Of course, but if I pay now, perhaps we can have New Year's Eve together in it?"

He knew I was going down, but he did not know I planned to go back tonight given the confirmation of the sale. I continued, "Pay the £1000 to me now, and I will agree." I hastily added, "In the flat of course." He looked at me with the eagerness of someone who was simply besotted by my middle-age beauty. My eyes and eyebrows seduced his money to my account within the blink of his iPad transferring it. We had all brought our iPads or computers to check all relevant queries or problems that may have occurred. In order to keep the conversation going I asked Rebecca what her colourful nails in white and blue meant, chevron style.

Triumphantly she stood up with one hand in a fist position.

"I had them done in the colours of Frodon for the King George. Blue and white suits me doesn't it?" She admired her nails. "Had a fiver each way and it won at 20/1. Bit risky as had them done before the race, but Bryony Frost and Frodon are glued together, a sight to behold."

"Like Paddington and marmalade." Pretty was on the ball.

David could not resist. "Like Mary and me to be." It was said with a dirty smile aimed straight at me. "I am waiting patiently."

"That came second," Rebecca suddenly remembered, "but I did not back that one."

A horse called Waiting Patiently did come second. Rebecca was in full race mode by now making us all laugh as she pretended to ride out the horse to victory as the horse came to the furlough pole, (rather than furlong) smacking the side of her bottom. Ricki Sunack had done a good job with his furlough and self-employment grants. It had not stopped me going out of business, but a lot were grateful for his efforts. As her exultations died down with the laughter I returned to my computer. I checked my accounts soon afterwards, and sure enough the £1000 credit was there. I was flabbergasted at the speed and keenness he showed. I realised another £1000 to share that cost was appropriate given our signed contract.

"Anyone got any Christmas jokes?" I asked in order to prolong our final get together. Donald was first in. "What does Prince Philip say to the queen after every Christmas lunch?"

He paused as we thought and finally rather amusingly putting his hands above his head like antlers, "How long are you going to reign, Dear?"

David was impressed and followed it with as good as an impersonation of Prince Charles as possible by saying "Mumsey, do not worry about the repairs at Windsor, the workmen are all corgi registered."

Pretty added, "What do Santa's little helpers learn at school?"

Once again, she waited a while.

"They learn the ELF-ABET."

Rebecca was like a coiled spring looking straight at David. "What does Santa do to filthy rich con men?"

David eyeballed her back and without a care in the world. "I do not know, what does Santa do to filthy rich con men like me?"

His air of authority and confidence defiantly seductive.

"He slays them," Rebecca said, clearly still at war with him. I decided to end the jokes there and then.

"I only have one bottle of prosecco to share around."

I was packed and ready to leave as soon as the final formalities had been confirmed. Donald opened the bottle as I got six glasses out that were staying in the house. I told Pretty she would have the keys and liaise with Percy to give to the new owners. That was going to be in the New Year now on a date to be decided. The atmosphere in the room was filled with nostalgia, decadence and intrigue.

The phone went.

I always felt happier as I could hear better on the house phone. It reminded me to ring straight after and cancel the line. They thought it might be the children. David is walking around the room with a swagger. Rebecca looked outside at the sleet. Donald and Percy were checking there iPads and Pretty was sat sipping her prosecco with her folders in front of her. I repeated several times "The house is mine, yes and the money has been transferred."

I looked at Pretty and Percy as they searched and then shrugged at each other not knowing what exactly I had bought. "Good, I will be over there to sign the documents this Thursday and move in the first week in January if possible." I got off the phone as Rebecca said a van had pulled up outside with "Removals Abroad/UK Specialists".

I took over the role of chairman then, "Please take your seats as I have good news, bad news and very bad news."

David's face was a picture of concern, as was the rest of them, except Rebecca who had hopes the bad news was for David.

"The good news is I have bought a house."

"The bad news is that it is between Etretat and Fecamp in northern France. Just spoken to the Notaire's office and the secretary says all is in order. I have another appointment in the morning of the 31st. You see I paid the 10% on the 23rd and now the balance has cleared. A spacious four-bedroomed for under £300,000 with the exchange rate. Money talks doesn't it. I aimed the last remark at the three men. "And now the very bad news for you David is the days of the week are Lundi, Mardi, Mercredi, Jeudi, Vendredi, Samedi and Dimanche. Not a single Y in the day and with easy access to the south of England." I paused for a moment as everyone was shell shocked. I moved the prosecco to my lips and drank the rest in one. I had to be strong and resilient. I shared my thoughts as a final act of my intelligence.

"House prices much cheaper and thanks to Brexit a better exchange with Torfx than my bank. I will have plenty of spare cash, as you boys say, it is only business, just in case British Nationals moving to France can do so before 31st December, au revoir."

Before I left, I got onto my computer. Booking.com came up with the availability at La Domain Saint Clair Le Donjon. It is an expensive hotel in Etretat famous for artists. John and I had stayed at this upmarket hotel. There is a beautiful golf course about half a mile away, an essential ingredient for our holidays. As I booked, I taunted David. "Thanks for the rent money, it will cover five nights." The problems at the ports with the lorries had meant booking any hotels or ferry crossings impossible. Now the Brexit deal was done there was huge relief everywhere. Rebecca looked in seventh heaven, well not exactly as it had been burnt down, sipping more prosecco and in stitches over David's dilemma. Pretty was speechless. Percy was checking the small print of our contract. Donald was quick to recognise the situation. He proposed a toast as I prepared to leave the room, to go to my overloaded little Renault Clio.

"To the finest con lady, I have ever met." Rebecca was first to acknowledge as surprisingly did David. Percy remarked that opposites attract so I was not suitable for David. Even I laughed. I smiled as they all raised their glasses.

Pretty spotted an opportunity. "You can sleep with me when there is an i in the day." David was alert now. "So, Friday's only?"

"Of course not, just take me to France."

It is strange how laughter can build up when disaster faced David. He had not drunk much, and it was just past 2pm. He became intoxicatingly drunk with giddy laughter as he realised the contract was now worthless. The money was mostly in my French bank account. He had been outwitted. Humour can be the basis of life but money talks. I walked out of the room and checked the removal people had the right address in France. They were busy loading and would store my furniture and await further instructions. I made sure my car started. It was full of diesel and MOT and insurance proof in the car. I walked back into my house for the final time. We had all been friends and had many good times, but life changes. I had to collect my computer and handbag, check again my passport was there. The Brexit deal had made life for me much easier. I rebooted the computer and checked the 11pm Newhaven to Dieppe for Tuesday December 29th. I had to pinch myself, tonight yes it was tonight. I filled in the details as it offered me Portsmouth to Caen, but I stuck with Newhaven. An overnight Cabin would be needed. I felt a surge of relief as I pressed "Pay Here" with no worries as cabins are thoroughly cleaned. An early morning arrival with all the checks gave me plenty of time to get to the hotel. I could see the house on the way which I had bought off the internet to fill in time. I noticed a confirmation email with any special requests from Domaine Saint Clair Le Donjon. Arriving after 11am I asked for lunch for one at 1pm and booked diner for 7.30pm. I was in control of my own destiny. The goodbyes were strained. I went round the table with my Covid negative test in my hand. I needed one within seventy-two hours of my ferry. That allowed them to kiss me or give me the elbow, so to speak. They all wished me luck and happiness.

David had the final words for me with admiration, hopefulness and lust in his eyes. "I love you more than ever."

Rebecca dived in, "No fool like an old fool."

"Time to go said Zebedee," I quoted a classic children's character. The feeling of freedom was wonderful. They all came to wave me off. I was sad but strangely happy. I had no remorse from doing what I had done to David. He still had plenty of money. He had a good sense of humour. He certainly needed it now. The car window was down in the cold December air as my Clio purred into life. The snow had missed the east and south east of England. I allowed plenty of time to get to Newhaven. The car window obeyed my command to keep me warm. The final words I heard made me laugh for a long time as David spoke to Pretty.

"Better buy a French map, do you fancy a holiday in northern France next year?"

Rebecca said, "Hope they still have the guillotine for him, come on, Percy, time to go home."

Printed in Great Britain
by Amazon

86836633R00045